ON LINE

CARTOON NETWORK®

THE POWERPUFF GIRLS™

GOOD MONSTER, BAD MONSTER

Based on
"THE POWERPUFF GIRLS,"
as created by Craig McCracken

**PRESS
CARD
HERE**

SCHOLASTIC Inc.

New York   Toronto   London   Auckland   Sydney
Mexico City   New Delhi   Hong Kong   Buenos Aires

ISBN 0-439-34436-0

Designed by Peter Koblish
Illustrated by Aristides Ruiz

12 11 10 9 8 7 6 5 4 3 2 1   2 3 4 5 6 7/0

Printed in the U.S.A.

First Scholastic printing, May 2002

It is a good thing The Powerpuff Girls live in Townsville.

Bam! Pow! Zap!

Blossom, Bubbles, and Buttercup take on every monster in town.

One day, a new monster came to town. *Brrring!* The hotline rang.

"It is the Mayor," said Blossom. "A monster is attacking Townsville!"

The Girls flew downtown.
The monster was making a lot of noise.

"Let's blast it, Girls!" Blossom said.

Blossom zapped the monster with a pink laser beam.

Bubbles zapped the monster with a blue laser beam.

Buttercup zapped the monster with a green laser beam.

But the monster did not fight back.

"Ouch! Please stop!" the monster yelled.

"What is wrong?" Buttercup asked the monster.

"My name is Pete," said the monster. "I come from Monster Isle. The other monsters sent me here to make a mess out of Townsville. But I do not want to. I want to be good!"

"What kind of monster wants to be good?" Buttercup asked.

"Not all monsters are bad," said Bubbles. "Maybe we can help Pete be good."

"We can try," Blossom said.
Bubbles was happy. She showed
Pete how to water flowers.
"Good monster!" Bubbles said.

Then Pete tried it.
He did it the monster way.
"No, Pete," said Blossom.
"Bad monster!"

Bubbles tried again. She showed
Pete how to push the swings.
"Good monster!" Bubbles said.

Bubbles tried again. She showed Pete how to help people cross the street.

"Good monster!" Bubbles said.

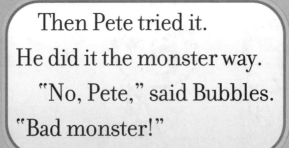

Then Pete tried it.
He did it the monster way.
"No, Pete," said Bubbles.
"Bad monster!"

Bubbles tried again. She showed
Pete how to paint.
"Good monster!" said Bubbles.

Then Pete tried it. He did it the monster way. "No, Pete," said Bubbles. "Bad monster!"

Bubbles did not give up.
She showed Pete how to clean.
"Good monster!" Bubbles said.

Then Pete tried it. He did it the monster way. "No, Pete," said Bubbles. "Bad monster!"

"That does it!" Buttercup yelled.
"Stop this right now!"
    "You have made a mess out of
Townsville," Blossom told Pete.

"Really? I made a mess out of Townsville?" Pete asked.

"That is right," Buttercup said.

"Hooray!" said Pete. "I made a mess out of Townsville. I can go home now."

Bubbles was sad. "But Pete, I know you can be good," she said.

"Maybe I can," said Pete.
"But I am still a monster."
The Girls waved good-bye
as Pete swam back to Monster Isle.

So once again, the day is saved . . . no thanks to a monster named Pete!